AMANDA & APRIL

Bonnie Pryor

Illustrated by Diane de Groat

William Morrow and Company, Inc.

New York

Library of Congress Cataloging-in-Publication Data
Pryor, Bonnie.   Amanda and April.   Summary: Amanda has many misadventures on the
way to Violet's party and discovers how really helpful her little sister April can be.
[1. Sisters—Fiction. 2. Behavior—Fiction. 3. Humorous stories] I. De Groat, Diane, ill.
II. Title. PZ7.P94965Am   1986   [E]   85-15308
ISBN 0-688-05869-8/ISBN 0-688-05870-1 (lib. bdg.)

AMANDA & APRIL

To Jenny and Chrissy

B.P.

One day an invitation came in the mail for Amanda.

Come to my house on Tuesday at two o'clock for my birthday. We will have chocolate cake.

— Violet

P.S. Bring April. She can play with my little brother Arthur.

"April can come, too," said Mrs. Pig. "How nice."

"How awful," said Amanda. "I wish I had a big sister. A big sister would take me for walks and show me how to play new games. A big sister would teach me how to whistle and blow bubbles with my gum. A little sister is no fun at all."

The day of the party, Mrs. Pig helped April put on her best dress.

"May we wear our new shoes?" asked Amanda.

"Yes," said Mrs. Pig. "If you promise not to step in any mud puddles."

Amanda promised she would be very careful. She put on her second-best dress with the pockets, and her new shoes and socks. Then Mrs. Pig helped her wrap the present for Violet. It was a puzzle with one hundred pieces that Amanda had picked out all by herself at the store.

"Don't forget to say thank you," Mrs. Pig said as they walked out the door. "And watch out for mud puddles."

Amanda looked up and down the street. "I don't see any mud puddles," she told April. "Watch me. I will show you how I can walk backward without even looking."

"You can't do it without peeking," said April.

"Oh, yes I can," said Amanda. She walked backward all the way to the corner. She only had to look once to see if there were any mud puddles, which didn't count, and once when she bumped into Mrs. Hog, which didn't count either.

"Look," said April when they reached the corner. Some men were fixing the street. The street was all covered with sticky black tar.

"What should we do now?" April asked. "How will we get to the birthday party?"

Amanda thought and thought. At last she had an idea. She took off her new shoes. Then she helped April take off her shoes, too. She carried the shoes to the other side of the street.

"Mama will be happy," Amanda said. "We did not get tar on our new shoes."

"Uh-oh," said April. She pointed to their new white socks. Amanda had forgotten to take them off and now they were covered with tar.

"Well," said Amanda. "Mama said to watch out for mud puddles. She did not tell us about gooey black tar."

Amanda took off their socks and put them in the pocket of her second-best dress. "We will carry our shoes the rest of the way," she said. "That way nothing can happen to them."

Amanda and April walked past a field full of pretty yellow flowers. "Let's pick some for Violet," Amanda said.

"I want to go to the party now," said April.

"It will only take a minute," Amanda said. "I will pick them very fast." She put the shoes and the gift on a rock and started to pick a big bunch of flowers.

Just then a bee flew by and landed on a flower. Amanda looked at the bee.

"I like bees," she said. "I am going to catch it."

"No," cried April. "Bees can sting." She tried to pull Amanda away from the bee.

"A big sister can teach you things," said Amanda. "I will teach you how to catch bees. You can do it when you are big like me."

Amanda found an old jar in the weeds. She put the jar over the bee and popped on the lid.

"Poor bee," said April, looking into the jar. "He doesn't look very happy."

Amanda looked at the bee. "I know what is wrong," she said. "That bee is lonesome." She caught three more bees to keep the first bee company.

"Now can we go to the party?" April asked.

Amanda carried the jar with the bees and the flowers for Violet to the rock where she had left the present. But something was wrong. The puzzle was gone and so were the shoes.

"Oh," said April. She looked ready to cry. "Now we can't go to the party. We don't have a present for Violet."

"Don't worry," said Amanda, "I will find it." She looked behind a tree and even under the rock, but she didn't find the present or the shoes.

Amanda saw a big white goat in a clump of weeds. He was chewing something with his big white teeth.

"Stop," yelled Amanda. "You are chewing Violet's present!"
She waved her arms and chased the goat to scare him away.
    The big white goat did run away. But he took one of
Amanda's shoes, and the present was torn. All of the puzzle
pieces were scattered on the ground.

April helped Amanda look for the pieces. They crawled through the bushes and looked in the weeds. Amanda tore the pocket of her second-best dress on a scratchy bush, but she didn't lose the socks. They were stuck to her dress by the gooey black tar.

Amanda sat down and counted the pieces. It took her a long time, but she did it.

"One piece is missing," she said sadly. "I hope Violet will like a puzzle with ninety-nine pieces."

It was getting late, and they were going to be late for the party. Amanda had to hurry. She opened the jar of bees to let them go free.

"Fly away, bees," she said. But one bee did not fly away. He fell to the ground and stung Amanda on her foot.

"Ouch," yelled Amanda. She didn't want to cry and have April think she was a baby, but she couldn't help it.

"Don't cry," said April. "I will help you." She tied her handkerchief around Amanda's foot. Then she helped Amanda hop on one foot all the way to Violet's house.

Everyone was already playing Pin the Tail on the Donkey when they got to the party. But Amanda could not walk on her hurt foot. She had to sit on a chair and watch. April brought her a glass of punch and a tissue to wipe her eyes.

Violet's mother called Mrs. Pig and asked her to come to the party. Mrs. Pig looked at Amanda's foot. She looked at her torn dress and the socks all covered with tar stuck to Amanda's second-best dress. Mrs. Pig put her head in her hands. She was very quiet.

"Don't be mad at Amanda," April said. "She was very careful about mud puddles."

Mrs. Pig began to laugh. At first it was only a chuckle, but soon she was laughing so hard that tears ran down her cheeks.

"I will stay and help with the party," she said. "Then we will all walk home together."

Amanda and April and Arthur helped Violet make the puzzle while Mrs. Pig helped Violet's mother in the kitchen. It was a good puzzle, even if it did only have ninety-nine pieces.

"I'm glad you are my sister," April said. "You taught me how
to catch bees and how to count all the way to ninety-nine."

Amanda put her arm around April. "I am glad you are my
sister, too. As soon as I learn how to blow bubbles with my
gum, I am going to teach you."